D1325861

RETURN TO THE LIBRARY OF DOOM

ZOMBIE IN THE LIBRARY

BY MICHAEL DAHL

ILLUSTRATED BY
BRADFORD KENDALL

Raintree

www.raintreepublishers.co.uk
Visit our website to find out
more information about
Raintree books.

To order:
☎ Phone 0845 6044371
📄 Fax +44 (0) 1865 312263
✉ Email myorders@raintreepublishers.co.uk

Customers from outside the UK please telephone +44 1865 312262

Raintree is an imprint of Capstone Global Library Limited, a company
incorporated in England and Wales having its registered office at 7 Pilgrim
Street, London, EC4V 6LB – Registered company number: 6695582

Art Director: Kay Fraser
Graphic Designer: Hilary Wacholz
Production Specialist: Michelle Biedscheid
Originated by Capstone Global Library Ltd
Printed in and bound in China by Leo Paper Products Ltd

ISBN 978 1 406 22505 1 (hardback)
15 14 13 12 11
10 9 8 7 6 5 4 3 2 1

ISBN 978 1 406 22512 9 (paperback)
15 14 13 12 11
10 9 8 7 6 5 4 3 2 1

British Library Cataloguing in Publication Data
A full catalogue record for this book is available from the British Library

Contents

Behold the Library of Doom! The world's largest collection of deadly and dangerous books. Only the Librarian can prevent these books from falling into the hands of those who would use them for evil.

ARE BOOKS ALIVE OR DEAD? OR ARE THEY SOMETHING ELSE . . . ?

Chapter 1

LIGHTNING

Adam stands on his front
porch and stares at the **STORM**.

BOLTS of electricity shoot from the sky.

Lightning **DANCES** along the horizon.

"It's alive!" says a woman's voice.

Adam's mother steps out on the porch.

She stands beside her son.

"It looks alive, doesn't it?" she says, staring at the **LIGHTNING**.

Adam nods.

"Sorry, Adam," she says. "It looks as though we're not going into town tonight."

"But the **SALE**..." Adam says.

"I'm sure the **library** will move their sale to tomorrow night," says his mother. "That storm is just too fierce," she adds. "Besides, don't you have enough books already?"

Chapter 2

MONSTER BOOK

Adam puts his hands in his pockets.

In one of his pockets, he can feel the pound **COINS** he's been saving.

£ £

He was planning to buy a special book for his mother's birthday.

Adam knows his mother likes books about old **MONSTER** films. Books like that are too expensive.

But a few days ago Adam was at the library.

He saw the **PERFECT** book for his mother.

The book was filled with **old** photos.

It had chapters on vampires, phantoms, werewolves, and zombies.

It had a photo from his mum's favourite **SCARY** film, *The Library of Doom.*

The hero was a monster hunter who wore dark glasses, even at night.

"Sorry, Adam," said a library worker.

"You can't **BORROW** that book. It's part of the sale we're having in a few days."

Sale? thought Adam. That was even better.

Now he could afford that **BOOK** for his mother's present.

"I'll put it aside," said the worker.

"You can buy it at the sale on Friday **NIGHT**."

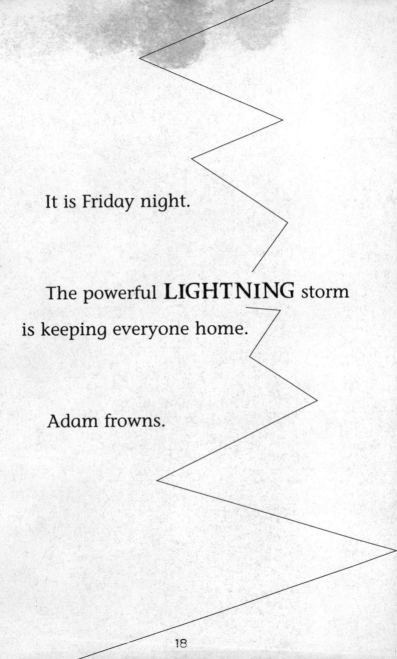

It is Friday night.

The powerful **LIGHTNING** storm
is keeping everyone home.

Adam frowns.

He supposes his mother is right.

No one will be at the town library tonight.

But Adam's mother is **WRONG**.

Chapter 3

THE UNWANTED

A shadow shuffles along the halls of the library.

The shadow is pushing a broom. It is Logan, the library's part-time caretaker.

Logan sees heaps of boxes sitting on several tables.

He **STOPS**.

"More rubbish!" he says to himself. "Why didn't someone tell me?"

The boxes are not rubbish. The books for tonight's sale are inside the boxes.

They were never unpacked. The librarian had left early because of the STORM.

Logan carries the heavy boxes outside.

He **HURLS** them into a big, metal wheelie bin, one by one.

The book that Adam wants to buy falls from a box.

It lands at the bottom of the bin.

It is buried beneath hundreds of other
used books.

Logan *throws* the last box into the

bin.

Then he pulls down the **HEAVY** metal

lid. "What a pain!" he says.

The lightning storm rages overhead.

Logan heads back towards
the **library**.

CRACK!

A bolt of lightning **HITS** the
metal wheelie bin.

A loud grinding noise **echoes** through the alley.

"What was that?" he yells. "Who's there?"

He sees steam **RISING** from the wheelie bin. Something is moving inside the bin.

Slowly, the metal lid rises.

Logan **screams**.

A book, shaped like a claw, is
lifting the lid.

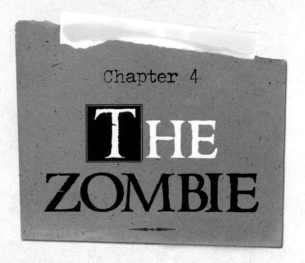

Chapter 4

THE ZOMBIE

Logan *runs* back inside the library.

From a window, he stares out at the wheelie bin.

A human-sized creature **CRAWLS** over the side of the bin.

The creature has no face. No eyes, no nose, no ears.

There is just a **HOLE** where its mouth should be.

The **CREATURE** reaches inside the
bin and pulls out a book.

It holds it up to the hole in its face.

Logan thinks the creature is
EATING the book.

The creature **pulls** out another book.

And another one.

It **CHEWS** at the books, and then tosses them aside.

Logan looks at the books that the creature has thrown away.

They are **SCATTERED** in the alley.

Lightning keeps flashing overhead.

Logan blinks his eyes. *I must be tired,* he thinks. *This can't be happening.*

Two of the books are **growing** legs.

SKINNY, papery legs sprout from the bottom of the book covers.

Thin arms are growing from the sides.

The living books **scuttle** towards the library.

Suddenly, the human-sized creature points at Logan.

The pages of its face **FLIP** angrily back and forth.

The creature roars.

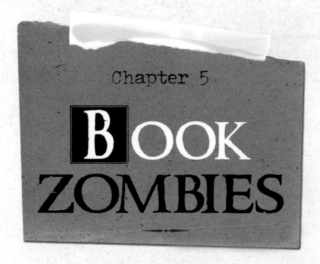

Chapter 5

BOOK ZOMBIES

Adam gets his bike out of the garage.

The lightning **won't stop** me from riding my bike, Adam thinks.

His bicycle's tyres are **RUBBER**. *Rubber tyres protect against electricity*, he tells himself. *Right?*

He is sure the **LIBRARY** will still have its sale.

*The **STORM** won't stop people who live in town*, Adam thinks.

And what if Mum's book is sold?

If I don't turn up **tonight***, the librarian might sell it to someone else.*

The library doors are **LOCKED** when he arrives.

There are lights on inside.

Adam **knocks**. No one answers.

Adam gets back on his bike. Maybe there is another door in the back.

As he turns into the alley, Adam runs into someone. "Sorry!" cries Adam.

Then he looks at the **STRANGER**.

The stranger has NO eyes. There is a book where its face should be.

The pages of the face **flip** open,
one by one.

Adam sees pictures of monsters.
Vampires. Phantoms. Werewolves.
ZOMBIES.

The creature holds its arms out. It
lunges towards Adam.

Adam hears a **screech** behind
him.

A pickup truck has turned into the alley. Logan is **GRIPPING** the wheel.

"Get in!" he yells at Adam.

Adam throws himself at the truck's door. He **LEAPS** inside.

The faceless creature **CLAWS** at the window.

The walking books begin climbing on to the back of the truck.

"Get off my truck!" yells Logan.

"We need to get out of here," whispers Adam.

Four more books **CLIMB** on to

the bonnet of the truck like fat spiders.

Chapter 6

LIGHTNING ROD

"I can't see where I'm going!"

Logan shouts.

The truck BOUNCES up and down.

"Oh no!" yells Adam. "That thing is in the back of the truck!"

A SHADOWY figure stands in the truck behind them.

Lightning **FLASHES** in the alley.

It was stupid to come here, Adam thinks to himself. *I should have listened to Mum. I should have come tomorrow. No book is worth this!*

A man's face presses against the back window.

The man wears **dark** sunglasses.

Adam recognizes him. It is the
same man from his mother's favourite
film.

It is the LIBRARIAN.

"Some books are worth it," says the man. "Now, hold on!"

Suddenly, white-hot **LIGHTNING** fills the air. A bolt of electricity shoots through the truck.

"Whoa!" yells Logan. "What's happening?"

Adam looks out of the back window. The **BOOK ZOMBIE** is gone.

The bed of the truck is full of ashy flakes, blowing in the wind.

Adam sees a <u>book</u> lying in the middle of the ashes.

The Librarian

It is his mother's book.

The wind *BLOWS* the pages
open to a photo.

It shows the hero from *The Library
of Doom* flying through the **SKY**.

In a **BLAZE** of lightning, Adam

sees the man with the sunglasses.

He is flying over the library.

"Rubber tyres," mutters Logan. "I think the rubber tyres **SAVED** us from getting fried."

Adam knows it was **MORE** than the tyres.

He feels the pound coins still in his pocket. He had saved up the money to buy his mother's present.

Tonight, his mother's present **SAVED** him.

AUTHOR

Michael Dahl is the author of more than 200 books for children and young adults. He has won the AEP Distinguished Achievement Award three times for his non-fiction. His Finnegan Zwake mystery series was shortlisted twice by the Anthony and Agatha awards. He has also written the Library of Doom series. He is a featured speaker at conferences around the country on graphic novels and high-interest books for boys.

ILLUSTRATOR

Bradford Kendall has enjoyed drawing for as long as he can remember. As a boy, he loved to read comic books and watch old monster movies. He graduated from university with a BFA in Illustration. He has owned his own commercial art business since 1983, and lives with his wife, Leigh, and their two children, Lily and Stephen. They also have a cat named Hansel and a dog named Gretel.

GLOSSARY

creature living being

electricity electrical power or current

fierce violent or dangerous; very strong or extreme

horizon line where the sky and the earth or sea seem to meet

lunges moves forward quickly and suddenly

protect guard or keep something safe from harm, attack, or injury

rages is violent or noisy

recognizes sees someone and knows who they are

rubber strong, elastic, and waterproof material used for making tyres, balls, boots, etc.

sprout start to grow

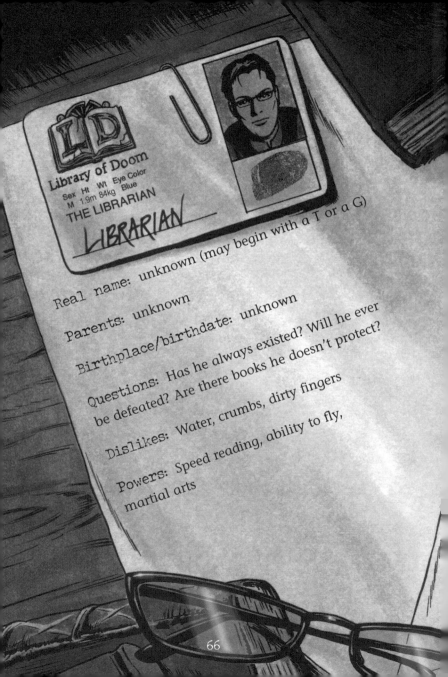

Library of Doom

Sex Ht Wt Eye Color
M 1.9m 84kg Blue

THE LIBRARIAN

LIBRARIAN

Real name: unknown (may begin with a T or a G)

Parents: unknown

Birthplace/birthdate: unknown

Questions: Has he always existed? Will he ever be defeated? Are there books he doesn't protect?

Dislikes: Water, crumbs, dirty fingers

Powers: Speed reading, ability to fly, martial arts

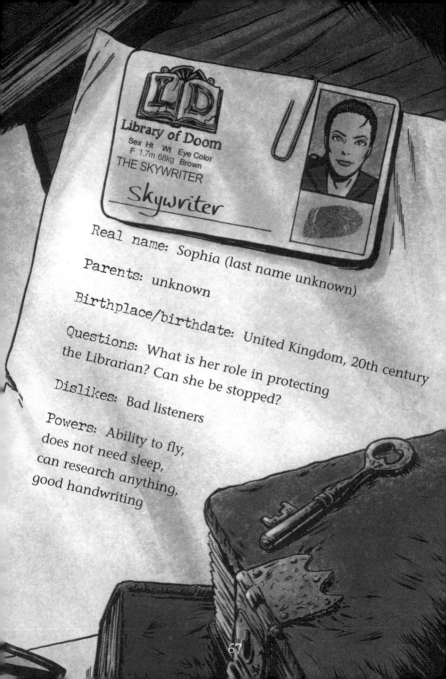

Library of Doom

Sex Ht Wt Eye Color
F 1.7m 68kg Brown
THE SKYWRITER

Skywriter

Real name: Sophia (last name unknown)

Parents: unknown

Birthplace/birthdate: United Kingdom, 20th century

Questions: What is her role in protecting the Librarian? Can she be stopped?

Dislikes: Bad listeners

Powers: Ability to fly, does not need sleep, can research anything, good handwriting

BOOK ZOMBIE

The Book Zombie that Logan and Adam encountered in the library was not the first Book Zombie to face the Librarian. In fact, dozens of Book Zombies have been spotted, often during thunderstorms or tornadoes.

Usually seen during large electrical storms, Book Zombies are known for their speed and fearfulness. It is not known why they emerge during thunderstorms. However, the only thing known to destroy them is a large bolt of electricity, such as lightning. When the Librarian can get there in time, he can harness the lightning and destroy the Book Zombie. But there will always be more . . .

DISCUSSION QUESTIONS

1. Do you think Adam will get in trouble for going to the library in the **STORM**? Why or why not?

2. What did you think about the title of this book? Does it match what you felt when you read the story? Can you think of other titles that would be a **GOOD** fit for this book?

3. Who is the Librarian? What is the Library of Doom?

WRITING PROMPTS

1. In this book, Adam is in a dangerous situation. Write about a time when you experienced **DANGER**.

2. Pretend you're Adam. Write a letter to a friend, explaining what happened at the library.

3. **CREATE** a cover for a book. It can be this book or another book you like, or a made-up book. Don't forget to write the information on the back, and include the author and illustrator names!

More books from the Library of Doom